Little Cottontail

By Carl Memling
Illustrated by Lilian Obligado

A GOLDEN BOOK • NEW YORK
Western Publishing Company, Inc., Racine, Wisconsin 53404

MCMXCV

Once there was a little cottontail rabbit who lived in a cozy nest.

"Mother," said the little cottontail, "when will I grow up?"

"Soon," said his mother.

"But first, Little Cottontail, you must leave the nest."

"Leave the nest?" he said.

His little round nest was just the right size. It was soft and warm, with a bed made of grass and tufts of fur. It was a nice nest.

A mother and a father robin peered down at him.
Their babies were still too young to leave the nest.
They wondered what Little Cottontail would do.

With a flop and a hop, and a hump and a bump,
Little Cottontail left the nest.

"NOW am I grown up?" he asked.

His mother smiled. "Not yet," she said. "First, Little Cottontail, you must learn to wash yourself."

"Please teach me," he said.

"Watch closely," said his mother.

A porcupine sitting on a hollow log watched closely, too.

"This is the way you wash yourself early in the morning.

"Shake your feet, one at a time. Then lick them clean, one at a time.

"Scrub your face with your little front paws.

"Scratch your ears with your big hind paws.

"Then fluff all your fur up and lick it clean—and you'll be bright and shining early in the morning."

"I can do all that," said Little Cottontail.

And he did.

"Didn't he do that very well!" a deer mouse
whispered to her tiny children.

"NOW am I grown up?" asked Little Cottontail.

"Not yet," said his mother.

"First, Little Cottontail, you must learn what big rabbits eat. . . .

"Out in the meadow all summer long, they eat grass and herbs and lots of green plants.

"Over by the farmhouse all summer long, they eat
carrots and cabbage and nice fresh fruit.

"All through the winter, white with snow, they eat
buds and twigs and the bark of trees.

"These are things that big rabbits eat whenever
they are hungry."

Little Cottontail said, "I listened closely, and I think I know them."

And he did.

"NOW am I grown up?" asked Little Cottontail.

"Not yet!" hissed a woodchuck, popping up from his burrow. "First, you must learn about foxes!"

"What about foxes?" said Little Cottontail.

"Foxes like to chase rabbits," said his mother. "They like to catch them for dinner.

"You must learn how to tell that a fox is coming. Please, Little Cottontail, watch very closely. . . .

"This is the way you twitch your nose—*sniff-sniff, sniff-sniff . . . sniff-sniff-sniff*—to sniff the air for the smell of a fox.

"And this is the way you cock your ears, and raise your head, and glance about—to see if that bad fox is coming near.

"And if the fox comes, this is the way you lay back your ears and bound away. This is the way you hop, hop, hop as fast as you can, before the fox can catch you.

"You dodge and you twist and you take shortcuts.

"You zigzag and circle and double back on your tracks.

"You lead the fox to a brier patch. You do a quick-quick stop there and hop to the side. You freeze like a statue—and the fox runs by.

"And all that the fox ever does catch is a pawful of thorns in the brier patch."

"That's so much to learn," said Little Cottontail, "though I did listen closely.

"Now, let me see. What came first? . . . Oh, yes. First, I must twitch my nose."

So Little Cottontail
twitched his nose to
sniff the air for the
smell of a fox. Then
he cocked his ears
and glanced about. . . .

"Mother!" cried Little Cottontail. "A FOX *IS* COMING!"

Into the hollow log sprang the porcupine. The deer mouse scampered off swiftly with her tiny children. Down popped the woodchuck into his burrow. And *"Chee-chee!"* cried the robin as he flew away.

Little Cottontail and his mother laid back their ears and bounded away—and the fox chased after them! "Oh, dear," thought the mother. "What if Little Cottontail doesn't remember all I told him?"

But Little Cottontail zigzagged

and circled

and

doubled back on his tracks.

And then he came to a quick-quick stop and hopped to the side.

He froze like a statue—and the fox ran by, straight into the thorns of a brier patch!

"Mother," said the cottontail, gasping for breath, "NOW am I grown up?"

"Yes," said his mother. "Now you are grown up—BIG COTTONTAIL!"